the Pagemaster™

CLASSIC SERIES

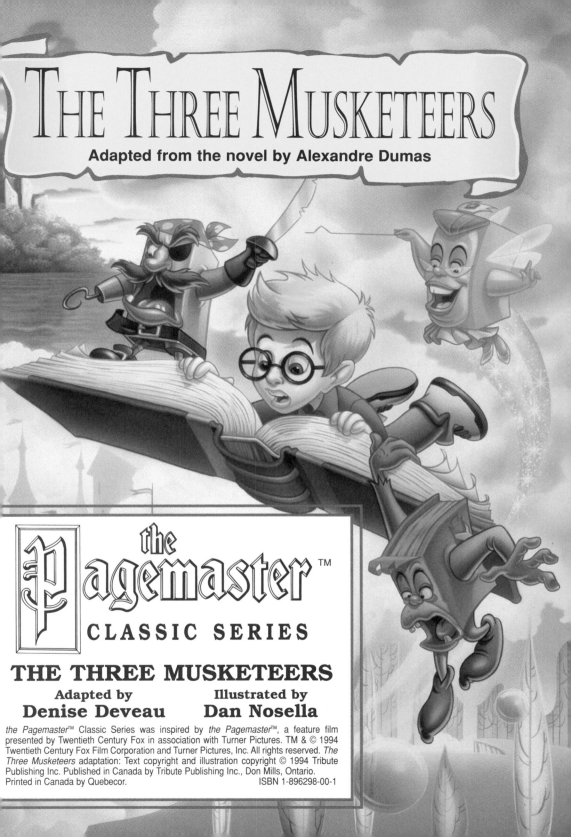

THE THREE MUSKETEERS

Adapted from the novel by Alexandre Dumas

the Pagemaster™

CLASSIC SERIES

THE THREE MUSKETEERS

Adapted by
Denise Deveau

Illustrated by
Dan Nosella

the Pagemaster™ Classic Series was inspired by the Pagemaster™, a feature film presented by Twentieth Century Fox in association with Turner Pictures. TM & © 1994 Twentieth Century Fox Film Corporation and Turner Pictures, Inc. All rights reserved. The Three Musketeers adaptation: Text copyright and illustration copyright © 1994 Tribute Publishing Inc. Published in Canada by Tribute Publishing Inc., Don Mills, Ontario. Printed in Canada by Quebecor.   ISBN 1-896298-00-1

the Pagemaster™

presents

THE THREE MUSKETEERS

Adapted from the novel by Alexandre Dumas

On a fine spring day in 1626, the people of Meung, a market town in France, were gathered outside an inn to view an unusual sight. A handsome young stranger in farmer's clothes had just arrived on an old and shabby yellow horse.

The young man was named D'Artagnan, and he wanted to make his fortune as a member of the king's Musketeers. The Musketeers were the guards of King Louis XIII and Queen Anne of France. They were also the enemies of the king's advisor, Cardinal Richelieu and his guards. Richelieu was a man who would do anything to gain power over the king.

D'Artagnan may have been brave, but he also had a short temper. As he got off his horse, D'Artagnan noticed three men. One was a tall man with a scar on his cheek. The gentleman with the scar was a close friend of the cardinal's. As the men talked, they laughed and pointed in D'Artagnan's direction.

"I say, sir," said D'Artagnan angrily. "Tell me what you are laughing at!"

The man looked at him and replied, "I was not speaking to you, sir."

"But I am speaking to you!" answered D'Artagnan.

"That horse looks like a buttercup," said the man to his friends as he turned away.

At that, everyone laughed and D'Artagnan could not control himself. He drew his sword. "Turn sir, or I will strike you from behind!" he shouted.

"Strike me?! You're mad!"

D'Artagnan lunged toward him. He stepped back. Then the man's friends got into the fight and attacked D'Artagnan with their hands. D'Artagnan was overpowered by his attackers and lost the fight.

Afterwards, D'Artagnan said, "We shall see what the captain of the Musketeers thinks of your insults. I have in my pocket a letter of introduction to the captain of the Musketeers."

Suddenly, the stranger looked very worried.

While D'Artagnan was being helped back up to his feet by the town innkeeper, the man with the scar turned his attentions to a lady who was watching from her carriage. She was a beautiful woman with long blonde hair, a lovely smile, and skin as white as alabaster. But her eyes were cold and cruel.

"Milady," the man whispered. "The cardinal has ordered you to return to England and let him know the moment the Duke of Buckingham leaves London. Here is a box with further instructions. Do not open it until you reach London. I shall return to Paris."

They headed off in opposite directions. D'Artagnan stayed the night at the inn. The next morning, he noticed that his letter of introduction from his father was gone!

"Where is my letter!" he cried. "It contained my future fortune."

immediately went to the home of the captain of the famed Musketeers, Monsieur de Treville. Treville was a great favourite of the king. The cardinal and his guards hated him and all his Musketeers.

D'Artagnan felt very nervous when he entered. The headquarters was full of Musketeers.

The innkeeper said, "The tall gentleman came back and was in the kitchen when you were in your room. You had left your vest there."

"Then he is the thief," said D'Artagnan. He decided then and there that he would have revenge on this strange man.

Little did he know that the man and Milady would become his mortal enemies in days to come. For now, however, D'Artagnan's mind was on other matters, and he made his way to Paris and the headquarters of the Musketeers.

On reaching Paris, D'Artagnan

He explained to the captain that his letter of introduction had been stolen. Just as the captain was about to write a letter to the director of another regiment admitting D'Artagnan for training, the young man dashed out of the room with a cry of, "There's the man who stole my letter! I shall take him!"

As he tore down the stairs, D'Artagnan ran head first into a very noble and handsome Musketeer with a wounded shoulder. His name was Athos.

"Watch what you're doing," called Athos. "You're very rude."

"I did not mean to do it," said D'Artagnan. "If I weren't in such a hurry I would fight you for your rudeness to me."

"I shall meet you tomorrow at noon in the next courtyard," said Athos. "We'll fight then."

"That will do fine," called D'Artagnan as he ran out.

In his haste, D'Artagnan sped past another Musketeer named Porthos. He was tall and richly dressed in a long red velvet cloak. D'Artagnan was in such a hurry he got tangled up in the Musketeer's cloak.

"You do not run into Musketeers in this way," said Porthos. "Meet me tomorrow at one o'clock and we shall settle the matter."

"One o'clock then," agreed D'Artagnan.

As he continued his chase, D'Artagnan realized that he had lost his man.

As he thought about his bad luck, D'Artagnan saw yet another Musketeer talking to some men. Aramis was his name. Aramis had dropped a handkerchief with initials on it, so D'Artagnan said as politely as he could, "Excuse me, sir, but you appear to have dropped your handkerchief."

Aramis glared at D'Artagnan angrily and replied, "You are mistaken. It is not mine."

The handkerchief belonged to a girlfriend of his who Aramis did not want his friends to know he was seeing.

"But I saw you drop it," he insisted.

"You are wrong," said Aramis.

"I saw it fall," said D'Artagnan again. "You are lying."

Aramis was now in a rage. "Meet me at two o'clock tomorrow and we will settle this matter."

D'ARTAGNAN'S FIRST DUEL

The next day, D'Artagnan came to the courtyard for his noon meeting with Athos. When he arrived, Athos was sitting on a wall waiting for him. "I am expecting my friends," said Athos. "We can begin then."

In a short time, Aramis and Porthos arrived. "What? Are these the friends you speak of?" exclaimed D'Artagnan.

"Yes indeed. Are you not aware that we are known as the Three Musketeers?" boasted Athos.

"But I am going to fight him at one o'clock," said Porthos.

"And I at two o'clock," added Aramis.

"Well, I hope you'll excuse me if

I can't make all these appointments," said D'Artagnan. "If I am killed now, then I cannot possibly keep my word. Now, Athos, on guard!"

Just as he drew his sword, a loud commotion began behind them. It was five of the cardinal's guards ready to attack the Musketeers.

"Now what will we do," pondered Athos. "They are five and we are only three."

"No, we are four," called D'Artagnan. "I shall join you. Try me."

"What is your name?" asked Athos.

"It is D'Artagnan."

"Well then D'Artagnan, let us fight."

The battle was not a long one.

D'Artagnan was not an experienced fighter, but he was so excited at the thought of being with the Musketeers, he easily beat the man who attacked him. The Musketeers were equally as fast in defeating the rest of the guards. Once it was over, the Musketeers introduced themselves by name and invited D'Artagnan to celebrate with them.

Together, the four men walked arm in arm down the street. D'Artagnan was beside himself with joy. He was a friend of the Three Musketeers!

THE FOUR FRIENDS

It was not long before the king heard of the fight between the Musketeers and the cardinal's guards.

King Louis was happy his men performed so well and offered D'Artagnan gold coins and a position as a cadet in the Company of the Guards. "I cannot wait to see the face the cardinal will make over this," laughed the king. "He will be furious."

D'Artagnan took his money and hired a servant named Planchet and found an apartment at the home of a Monsieur Bonacieux.

During his first few days in Paris, he spent his time getting to know his new-found friends. He learned that Athos, the eldest of the three, had a great mystery in his past that he would not talk about.

Porthos, on the other hand, talked a lot to anyone who was there, whether they were listening or not. He also spent much of his money on splendid clothes and gambling.

As for Aramis, he was a simple man and asked for little. However, he always seemed to have something to do, so was not around very often.

The four men became such good friends when D'Artagnan began his service as a cadet, Athos, Porthos and Aramis joined the same guard to be with him.

THE LANDLORD'S WIFE

One day, D'Artagnan was visited by his landlord, Monsieur Bonacieux.

"I have come to see you, Monsieur D'Artagnan, on an important matter," he said. "My wife, Constance, who is a seamstress to the queen, was kidnapped yesterday. She was taken by a man with a scar. I think it was because she may have helped arrange meetings between the queen and the Duke of Buckingham.

"Just a few days ago, the queen told my wife that someone had written to the duke in the queen's name to trick him into coming to Paris," he continued. "I do not care so much for Constance, but if she is in trouble, then I am sure to be suspected. Please help me."

"Leave this with me," said D'Artagnan.

Soon after, the three Musketeers arrived for a visit and he told them all that had happened.

"I have heard it said that the queen loves the Duke of Buckingham," said D'Artagnan.

"I have also heard that he is worthy of her love," noted Athos. "He is noble and kind. But is it true that he is in Paris because of a false letter?"

"The queen is afraid so," said D'Artagnan. "We must find the landlord's wife. She holds the key to the whole mystery."

Just then the door of his room was thrown open and the landlord came in and cried, "Save me! They have come to arrest me!" Four guards grabbed him by the arms and took him away.

"For now, Bonacieux is safer in jail than in this house," said D'Artagnan. "Now, gentlemen, on with our mission. All for one and one for all. That shall be our motto. And from this moment on, we are enemies of the cardinal."

"All for one and one for all!" shouted the four men together.

MEETING CONSTANCE

For a while, the landlord's house was taken over by the cardinal's people. D'Artagnan heard loud cries coming from downstairs.

He heard a lady say, "But I tell you that I live here! I am the landlord's wife and seamstress to the queen."

What a stroke of luck, thought D'Artagnan. The woman I am looking for.

D'Artagnan sprang into action. He lowered himself to the first floor from his window and rushed into the room with his sword in his hand. There he was confronted by three of the cardinal's men brandishing swords of their own. After a lot of crashing and clashing of swords, D'Artagnan drove the three men out of the room in fear of their lives.

D'Artagnan was alone with Constance Bonacieux. He was surprised by how beautiful she was, with her long dark hair, blue eyes and sweet smile. He noticed that an unusual handkerchief with initials was lying at her feet. He gallantly picked it up and returned it to her.

"Ah kind sir, you have saved me," she said, as she placed the item in her pocket. "But what could these men want with me? And where is my husband?"

"He has been taken to the Bastille," replied D'Artagnan.

"But he is innocent!"

"He will be safe in time," said D'Artagnan. "Please, tell me how you managed to escape from your kidnappers."

"When they left me alone for a moment, I let myself down from a window," she explained. "I came straight here to find my husband so I could send him on an errand."

"And what was that?"

"Can I depend on you?"

"Gladly, madame. How can I help you?"

"Go to the Louvre where the queen lives and ask for her valet. When he comes to speak to you, send him to me."

"Consider it done," assured D'Artagnan.

D'Artagnan delivered Constance to a safe hiding place and carried out her orders. Then D'Artagnan returned home with thoughts of the lovely Constance in his head.

LEARNING A SECRET

On his way back from the Louvre, D'Artagnan decided to visit Aramis. As he turned down the street, he saw a woman in a long cloak tapping on the window of a house. The shutters opened and the woman handed the person a handkerchief. It was exactly like the one that D'Artagnan had returned to Constance.

As the lady turned to leave, D'Artagnan saw to his amazement that it was Constance! He stepped forward to speak to her. In her fright, she fell to the ground and cried out, "Kill me if you must, but I shall tell you nothing."

When she realized who it was, she said. "Oh, thank goodness it is you! But why are you following me?"

"I was on my way to visit my friend and I saw you at this house. I waited to see what you were doing."

"I cannot tell," she whispered. "However, please help me by walking with me to another house where I must deliver a message by midnight. But you must promise not to ask me anything and you must leave before I enter the house."

He did as she asked then continued on his course, stopping to talk to some people on the street along the way. In a short time he came to the top of a set of stairs. At the bottom, he saw a man dressed as a Musketeer and a woman ahead of him. It was Constance!

D'Artagnan was furious. He was certain Constance had lied to him and was meeting secretly with one of his friends. He ran down the stairs and blocked their passage.

"What do you want, sir?" asked the man, who spoke with an English accent.

D'Artagnan was stunned. He was not looking at a Musketeer, but at the Duke of Buckingham, minister to the King of England! Constance stepped between the two men and implored D'Artagnan to let them pass.

"I am so sorry. I thought you were someone else," he apologized. "Is there any way I can be of service to your grace?"

The duke replied, "You are a brave young man and I accept

your services. We are on our way to the Louvre. Make sure no one follows us."

THE DUKE AND THE QUEEN

As an enemy of the king of France, the duke had risked his life to come to Paris. He knew the letter he had been sent was not really from the queen, but he came to her anyway, because he loved her more than any other woman in the world.

The Duke of Buckingham was considered by many to be the most handsome man in England. He was admired by his English king, his countrymen and the Queen of France.

When Queen Anne arrived, she was dazzling. The duke was speechless. As she stepped forward, he fell to his knees and kissed her hand.

The queen looked at him sadly. "Don't you understand that we can never be together? I am married to the King of France and England is our enemy. Everything separates us. Our countries are at war and my husband already suspects you."

"I cannot bear to think that we must be separated forever," cried the duke. "I would risk anything to be with you again. I ask for nothing more than that you love me in return."

"I would go mad if I were to be the cause of your death in France. I beg you to go back to England now, so I can rest easy," she pleaded.

"I will do as you ask, I swear. But I must have something to remember you by."

The queen left her chamber and returned with a rosewood box. "Here, my Lord. Take these 12 diamond studs and keep them in memory of me."

He left with a final bow and a kiss of her hand, taking the diamond studs with him.

A CONSPIRACY

During the time that D'Artagnan and Constance were having their adventure, the landlord, Constance's husband, was having one of a very different kind. The officers who arrested him took him straight to the Bastille where he was thrown in a cell and questioned by soldiers.

"But I know nothing," he said many times. "I have no idea what my wife has done. She means nothing to me. As to the man who kidnapped her, I do not know him either!"

The next night he found himself face to face with Cardinal Richelieu himself.

"I see you are accused of high treason," said the cardinal in a commanding voice.

The landlord trembled with fear. "I swear I know nothing."

Aloud he said, "You have plotted with your wife and the Duke of Buckingham."

"Indeed sir, I have not. I did hear her say that the cardinal had tricked the duke into coming to England. But I told her that the cardinal was not capable of such a..."

"Silence," shouted the cardinal. "You are a stupid man."

"That's what my wife says to me all the time, your eminence," agreed the landlord.

"Do you know where your wife is now?"

"Absolutely not! I have been in jail." Bonacieux was shaking.

"Trust me, we shall know all," said the cardinal. "First, you must tell us everything you know of your wife's movements in the past few days."

Bonacieux told the cardinal more than he needed to know.

When the cardinal was satisfied, he shook Bonacieux's hand, gave him some gold coins and said, "Go my friend."

Bonacieux jumped for joy. "What an excellent man you are, sir. You are a man of genius and I am your servant."

While the landlord was enjoying his good fortune, the man with the scar arrived with important news for the cardinal.

"A servant has informed me that the queen and the duke have seen each other," he said eagerly.

"The queen presented the duke with the diamond studs that were given to her by the king."

"Excellent," smiled the cardinal. "We have her now. Send for my servant. I have an important message to deliver."

"And the landlord?" asked the man.

"I have made sure that he will spy on his wife."

When the man left, the cardinal wrote a letter that said:

"Milady — Be at the first ball where the Duke of Buckingham will be present. He will wear 12 diamond studs. Get as near to him as you can and cut off two. Once you have them, let me know immediately."

"Go with all speed and deliver this to Milady in London," he ordered the messenger.

THE QUEEN'S PROBLEM

The cardinal was ready to set in motion his plan to ruin the queen. His hatred for the queen and the Duke of Buckingham surprised those who knew him. But the cardinal had his reasons. He once loved the queen and was rejected in favour of the duke. Since that time, he vowed he would do all he could to destroy them both.

The first step in his plan was a visit to the king. "Sire, I have heard that the Duke of Buckingham is in Paris."

"What! Here!" exclaimed the king. "What for?"

"No doubt to plot with your enemies," replied the cardinal. "Perhaps even the queen."

"Do you really think so?" asked the king. King Louis was always ready to believe that his wife was up to something behind his back.

A week later, the cardinal received a letter from Milady: "I have the studs. I will be in Paris as soon as I can."

Now it was time for the cardinal to move into action. His next step was to convince the king to hold a fancy dress ball in two weeks.

As he and the king were planning the ball, the cardinal said casually, "Why don't you tell the queen to wear her diamond studs? They do become her so well."

The king was surprised by the cardinal's request, but he went to the queen anyway. "Madame, I wish to hold a ball in two weeks and, to honour the occasion, I would like you to wear the diamond studs I gave you on your birthday."

"Yes, your majesty," she answered. But she turned as white as a ghost. She knew right away that the cardinal was behind all of this.

Later, sitting alone in her room, she was heartbroken. "What am I to do?" she said out loud to herself.

It did look very bad indeed. Buckingham had returned to England and she could trust no one to speak to him.

"Can I help?" asked Constance, who had heard the queen's lament as she entered the room.

"You! Can I confide in you?"

"Indeed you can, my queen. Madame, you gave those studs to the duke, did you not? We must have them back."

"But how?" cried the queen.

"I know a messenger we can trust," said Constance.

"I shall write a letter for your messenger to take to London," said the queen. "It is addressed to Buckingham himself."

Constance raced home with the letter. She had no idea that her husband had become a spy for the cardinal. The poor woman mistakenly believed that he would be her messenger.

"I have something important to tell you," she whispered to her husband on her arrival. "You must deliver a paper to someone in London. There is much money in it for you."

"Much money?" The landlord's eyes lit up for he was a greedy man. "How much? And what is this letter all about? Who is this for?"

"An important person," she answered.

"Ah, I see. The cardinal warned me about things like this."

"You have seen the cardinal?" she gasped.

"Yes," he said with pride. "And he called me his friend."

Constance knew then that her husband could not be trusted.

"Perhaps this is not so important," she said casually. "I will give it up for now. Please say no more about it."

Bonacieux realized that he had made a mistake. He could have found out more if he had played along with her. "By the way, I have to meet a friend," he said nervously. "But I'll be back soon." At that he left to inform the cardinal of his wife's plans.

"Now what can I do?" sighed Constance.

"Dear Madame," came a voice from beyond the door. "I will help you." It was D'Artagnan.

"Oh kind sir, you heard what was said?" she asked, as she opened the door.

"Everything, Constance. And I know you need a devoted and loyal man to make a trip to London. I am your man."

"Can I trust you?"

"Madame, can you not see that I love you and that I am loyal to my queen? This journey will prove it to you."

Constance gave him the letter. "Hurry then! There is very little time."

"I go at once," said the brave D'Artagnan. He left by the back door at the same time that the landlord returned with the man with the scar.

"Bonacieux," scolded the man. "You were a fool not to have pretended to accept the job. You would then have the letter. See if you can get it."

But it was too late. D'Artagnan was on his way to London to see the Duke of Buckingham.

THE JOURNEY TO LONDON

D'Artagnan went straight to Athos, Porthos and Aramis for help on his mission. "Gentlemen,

we ride for London, tonight," he told his astonished friends.

"Why are we going?" asked Porthos.

"I cannot tell you," answered D'Artagnan. "You must trust me and ask no further questions. I tell you only that I have a letter that must be delivered to the Duke of Buckingham."

"All for one and one for all," they cried out in unison.

The four men left Paris at two in the morning. Six hours later they arrived in a town where they stopped at an inn for breakfast. After they sat down to eat, a surly looking stranger at the next table asked Porthos to drink to the cardinal's health. Porthos, in turn, asked the man to drink a toast to the king.

"I serve no man but the cardinal," shouted the man and he drew his sword.

"Take care of this fellow, Porthos, and join us as soon as you can," ordered Athos.

The remaining three men carried on their journey as Porthos stayed behind to fight the stranger. Two hours later, after resting awhile, they saw eight men working on a road. As they rode nearer, the men drew out their muskets and began to shoot at the travellers. Aramis was hit in the shoulder.

"It's an ambush!" shouted D'Artagnan. "Ride like the wind!"

They managed to outfox the ambush and continue on their way to England. But, at the next town, Aramis was too weak to carry on, so they left him at a local inn to recover.

Now only Athos and D'Artagnan were left. At midnight they came to a village, where they decided to sleep. The next morning when they came to pay their bill, the landlord of the inn took the money and suddenly cried out that the money was fake and that they would be arrested. As he said this, four men with weapons came in and attacked them.

"I am wounded," Athos called to D'Artagnan during the battle that ensued. "Leave me here."

D'Artagnan had no choice. "I shall come back for you," he shouted as he fought his way out of the inn.

He galloped full speed to Calais where he boarded a boat for England. The next morning he was in Dover. He then rode as fast as he could to reach London and the duke's residence. When the Duke of Buckingham saw D'Artagnan, he rushed to him and asked, "Nothing has happened to the queen I hope?"

"Not yet," said D'Artagnan. "But I believe she is in danger and you are the only person who can save her. Take this letter. It will explain everything."

The duke read the letter and then grabbed D'Artagnan by the arm. "Come, we have a job to do."

He led D'Artagnan to a secret room. "Here," he said. "These are the jewels the queen is desperately looking for."

As he handed the box to D'Artagnan, he let out a cry. "All is lost! Two of the studs are missing! There are only 10. They have been stolen. I was at a ball where Milady, or should I say the Lady de Winter, danced with me. She must have taken them then."

The duke thought for a moment. "I will pay my jeweller twice the value of the studs to replace them in time for the ball."

The two studs were replaced in time, and D'Artagnan sped to Dover, where the duke had arranged for a ship to take him to France. When he landed in France, he rode non-stop until he reached Paris.

THE QUEEN IS SAVED

The next day, the ball was the talk of Paris. When the queen arrived, she was not wearing her diamond studs.

"Why are you not wearing your jewels?" demanded the king.

"I was afraid they would be damaged," she replied.

The king shook with rage. "You were wrong. I gave you those diamonds so that you would wear them. I demand that you get them at once."

While she was out of the room, the cardinal presented the king with two diamond studs.

"If the queen has the studs, which she probably does not, count them," said the cardinal with a smile. "If you find only 10, ask her who could have stolen two?"

The men heard the crowd gasp. The queen had returned in a magnificent costume. Around her neck sparkled the diamond studs.

The king was delighted, but the cardinal was white with rage. The king then saw that she had 12 diamond studs around her neck. None were missing. "What does this mean, cardinal?" the king asked.

The cardinal had to think fast. "This means that I wanted to present a gift to the queen of these two studs," he answered as politely as he could.

"I am grateful," said the queen as she looked knowingly at the cardinal. "I know these two studs cost you dearly."

The day after the ball, the queen sent for D'Artagnan and rewarded him handsomely for his brave deeds.

NEW ADVENTURES

D'Artagnan arrived home one evening to find a note under his door. "Be in front of the pavilion at St. Cloud at 10 o'clock," it said. D'Artagnan was overjoyed. It was from Constance.

At St. Cloud, he waited for more than an hour, but she did not come. He climbed a wall to look into the window of the pavilion and saw that the room was in a turmoil. What worried D'Artagnan most of all was a woman's torn glove that he found in the grass.

D'Artagnan asked everyone who lived nearby what they had seen. From them he found out that a young woman had been taken away by force by four men. D'Artagnan realized from their descriptions that one of the men was Bonacieux himself and that the leader was the infamous man with the scar!

D'Artagnan was beside himself with worry. He knew it was time to find his three friends and left the city at full gallop.

Porthos and Aramis were resting at the inns where D'Artagnan had left them.

At the third inn, he found Athos in quite a state. He had spent his time drinking and threatening anyone who came near him.

When Athos saw D'Artagnan, he invited him to join him. But too much wine and too little sleep had left their marks. Athos began to tell D'Artagnan the secret from his past.

"I want to tell you a story of how a woman has ruined my life," he said.

"I was once a wealthy man who fell in love with a girl of 16. She was so beautiful, I was blind to her faults. She had come to our town with her brother, a priest. Or so we thought."

"I married the girl. But I soon found out that she was not what she appeared to be. One day, I noticed she had a fleur-de-lis branded on her shoulder — the sign of a criminal. Worse yet, the man she claimed was her brother was her lover and a murderer. I will say no more except that I renounced her and left her for dead.

"Take heed my friend," he warned D'Artagnan. "People are not always what you think they are."

D'Artagnan and the Musketeers returned to Paris together. On his arrival, D'Artagnan had a letter from Treville telling him that the king was ready to begin a military campaign. He promised that D'Artagnan should enter the company of the Musketeers.

D'Artagnan was full of joy over the news. Finally, his dream to become a Musketeer had come true. The four friends went out to celebrate his new found success.

D'ARTAGNAN MEETS MILADY

As time went by, D'Artagnan found out that his beloved Constance had been taken to prison. The queen promised him she would do what she could to free her and place her safely in a convent.

The next day, as he and his servant passed by a church, D'Artagnan once again saw Milady pass by quickly in her carriage. He was determined to find out more about her. As luck would have it while riding their horses, D'Artagnan and his servant saw her carriage again that day. It was in front of the home of the Comte de Wardes, a man D'Artagnan had wounded in a duel.

It was there that D'Artagnan's servant intercepted a letter from Milady addressed to the Comte de Wardes.

D'Artagnan seized the letter and read: "I need to know when I can see you. Please send me word tomorrow."

Ah! Could Milady be in love with this de Wardes, he wondered. He followed her carriage for a while until it stopped. He could see Milady arguing with a man on the road.

"Madame," said D'Artagnan, as he stepped forward. "Say one word, and I shall take care of this man for you."

Milady turned in surprise. "Monsieur, I would be glad of your help if this man were not my brother-in-law."

"I am sorry, Madame, I did not realize," he replied. He turned to the man and said, "And what is your name, sir?"

"I am Lord de Winter," he answered in an English accent. "Who is this stupid fellow?" he asked Milady.

"Sir, you may be the lady's brother-in-law, but you are no brother-in-law of mine," answered D'Artagnan. "On guard!"

"I am not armed at the moment," said Lord de Winter, who was now in a rage. "Meet me this evening at the inn and we shall settle this quarrel."

D'Artagnan could have easily won the duel that ensued later that evening, but he spared Lord de Winter's life in return for an introduction to Milady.

That evening, D'Artagnan paid a visit to the beautiful and mysterious Milady. He was charmed by her graceful manners and winning smile.

As they talked, D'Artagnan found out that Milady's husband was the brother of Lord de Winter. And that after her husband died, she became the sole heiress to her brother-in-law's fortune. Despite all the warnings, D'Artagnan was attracted to Milady. She invited him to return and visit her every evening.

He was shown out by her maid, Kitty, who seemed to like the handsome visitor. He did not know it yet, but Kitty would prove to be a valuable friend.

D'ARTAGNAN IS DECEIVED

D'Artagnan began to fall in love with Milady as he saw more and nore of her. This worried Kitty, vho knew her mistress all oo well.

One evening, Kitty took D'Artagnan aside upon his arrival und led him up a dark, winding staircase to her room. "I have a etter here that you should see." She handed it to D'Artagnan.

D'Artagnan read the note: "You nave not answered my first note. Have you forgotten me? You have a chance now to respond," the note said.

D'Artagnan turned pale. It was addressed to the Comte de Wardes! So she is in love with him after all — but not with me, he thought to himself.

"You are upset, Monsieur?" asked Kitty.

"Yes, but do not pity me," said D'Artagnan. "Instead, help me in planning my revenge. I will win her over and replace her rival!"

Their conversation was stopped by the sound of a door closing. "Wait!" warned Kitty. "She is coming to her room. Hide yourself!"

Kitty dashed out to answer Milady's bell. From his hiding place in the closet, D'Artagnan could hear everything they said to each other.

"I have not seen D'Artagnan this evening," said Milady. "He must be delayed. How I detest that man! He spared Lord de Winter's life in a duel and robbed me of my inheritance! I should have killed him long ago.

"Leave me now," she said to Kitty impatiently. "And make sure that you get me an answer to the letter I gave you for the Comte de Wardes."

What an evil woman, said D'Artagnan to himself. He now knew he had to seek revenge. Before he left, he made Kitty promise to give him Milady's next letter to de Wardes, which she did the following morning.

It said: "This is the third time I write to you to tell you I love you. Beware if you do not answer. Give your answer to the maid who bears this letter."

D'Artagnan took a pen and wrote: "Madame — I was not sure if you had sent the first two letters to me. But now I believe in your kindness. I will come and ask my pardon this evening at 11 o'clock. From the happiest of men, Comte de Wardes."

The letter was delivered to Milady who was overjoyed to

receive it. She ordered all the lights to be out when the Comte arrived so he could not be seen. This helped D'Artagnan carry out his plan.

D'Artagnan arrived disguised as the Comte and stood in the door-way to Milady's room. Milady spoke: "Comte de Wardes, why do you not enter? You know I wait for you. I am happy in the love you offer me and as a token of my love I give you this." She slipped a ring onto D'Artagnan's finger. It was a magnificent sapphire surrounded by diamonds. They arranged to meet again in a week.

The next day, D'Artagnan went to seek advice from Athos. After he told him everything that had passed with Milady, he showed him the ring Milady gave him. Athos turned deathly pale.

"That was from Milady?" he cried out. "That is impossible! This is the ring I gave my wife many years ago. But she is dead. D'Artagnan, take my advice. Stay away from this woman. Something tells me she is very dangerous for all of us."

"You're right," said D'Artagnan, who was concerned by Athos's reaction. "I will have done with her immediately."

D'Artagnan returned to his apartment and wrote another false letter from the Comte de Wardes saying he could not see her again.

When Milady received the letter she was furious. "When I am insulted I avenge myself," she said. She turned to Kitty. "Send for D'Artagnan, now!"

When D'Artagnan received the summons, he thought, "I must go to her, or she will suspect that something is wrong."

As the evening wore on, she became more charming. In time the conversation turned to matters of romance. "Do you love me?" she asked him.

D'Artagnan decided to play along. "From the moment I saw you," he said.

"What would you do to prove your love for me?"

"Anything, Milady."

"Then I ask you to kill a man that has offended me," she demanded. "His name is de Wardes."

"I will avenge you," he said. "Tomorrow is the day." With those words, D'Artagnan started to leave Milady's company.

"Wait!" she called after him. "What is that ring you have?"

D'Artagnan had forgotten he still had the sapphire with him. He realized he had no choice but to tell her everything. "Madame. It was I who came to you as the Comte de Wardes. You gave me the ring."

Pale and trembling, Milady looked like a mad-woman. She grabbed for his hand, but as she did so, the shoulder of her dress slipped. D'Artagnan was astonished to see a fleur-de-lis tattoo on her shoulder!

"Great heavens," he cried.

Milady was like an angry tigress. "You have my secret!" she screamed at him. "You shall die for this!" She grabbed a knife from her night table.

D'Artagnan was terrified by her anger. As he raced out of the room, Milady chased after him with the blade held high and her eyes blazing with hatred. When he slammed the door of the room behind him, he heard Milady stabbing the door again and again.

THE MUSKETEERS GO TO BATTLE

D'Artagnan rushed to Athos to tell him what happened. "Milady has a fleur-de-lis on her shoulder! Are you sure the woman you knew was dead?" he asked him.

"Is she fair, with blonde hair

and blue eyes? And is the fleur-de-lis a rose colour?" inquired Athos.

"Yes. Oh Athos! She will have her revenge on all of us."

"But how can this be?" Athos muttered. "I fear you may be right but I don't know how it can be so."

He shook his head and spoke again to D'Artagnan. "Take great care, D'Artagnan," warned Athos. "She is an agent of the cardinal who hates you for retrieving the diamond studs."

Athos stopped himself and laughed. Placing his hand on D'Artagnan's shoulder, he said, "Let us forget her for now. We have a campaign to think about. The day after tomorrow we have orders to join the battle at Rochelle."

At Rochelle, the battle waged for many days. D'Artagnan often spent time reflecting on his problems when he was alone in the camp. Constance had disappeared and the cardinal was his sworn enemy.

D'Artagnan did not yet know how far Milady would go to get her revenge. One evening, when he was with the Musketeers, he talked about his fears. After some time, he said to Athos, "The more I think about it, the more I am convinced that Milady is your wife."

"Perhaps. I cannot carry on like this without finding out," Athos replied. "It is time we solved this mystery once and for all."

The other Musketeers were delighted to join D'Artagnan and Athos in their quest.

TWO CONVERSATIONS

On their journey, they passed by an inn called the Red Dovecot. To their surprise, they saw the cardinal's horse in the courtyard! Athos asked the innkeeper if anyone else had arrived in the past few hours.

"Yes, sir. A fine young lady arrived in a carriage and immediately went to her room upstairs where the cardinal has joined her."

The Musketeers were in luck. They ordered their dinners and sat down at a table to discuss their plans. Suddenly they heard a woman's voice say, "I am listening, cardinal."

Athos started. He knew that voice. As he looked about he saw that there was a broken stovepipe that carried the voices from upstairs.

"A boat is sailing to England tomorrow," he heard the cardinal say. "You will go to London and see Buckingham. Tell him I will ruin the queen if he does not stop this war."

"And if he does not give in?" asked Milady.

"Then he must die," said the cardinal. "Perhaps a young man who falls in love with a beautiful woman might be persuaded to do the task."

"I am sure that lady can be found," said Milady coolly. "But she would have some requests to make of the cardinal first."

"Tell me what you wish," demanded the cardinal.

"I wish to know the convent where I can find the landlord's wife. Second, I wish to see D'Artagnan destroyed with your full pardon."

"It shall be done," said the cardinal.

Athos did not need to hear more. He waited for the cardinal to leave, then sent D'Artagnan, Porthos and Aramis on their way.

When they left, he proceeded up the stairs to Milady's room, covering his face with his hat and cloak.

"Who are you and what do you want?" she cried when she saw him.

"Do you not know me?" he asked, as he showed his face.

Milady gasped.

"Yes Milady, your husband in person."

Milady was so filled with terror she was speechless.

"You are a demon of the worst kind," said Athos. "I thought I had crushed you but you seem to have risen from the dead. I know much about you since you joined the cardinal. I also know you are planning to assassinate the duke and my friend D'Artagnan. Do not, if you value your life!"

"Hand me the paper the cardinal has given you or I shall kill you here and now," he demanded.

Milady gave Athos her letter of pardon. It read: "The crimes of the bearer of this letter were done by my order for the good of the State. Cardinal Richelieu."

Athos took the letter with him, leaving Milady in stunned silence. But Milady was not to be deterred so easily. In the morning she was on her way to England to plot the murder of the noble Duke of Buckingham.

MILADY IN ENGLAND

Athos rejoined his companions at Rochelle. "Gentlemen, it is time we had a meeting."

They sat together as Athos prepared to tell them of his encounter with Milady and discuss their plan to save the duke.

"First we must send a letter to Lord de Winter to detain Milady when she arrives," said Athos. "She must, under no circumstances, be allowed to go near the duke. De Winter is a close friend of the duke's and will make sure she cannot carry out her evil deed!"

D'Artagnan wrote the letter himself. It said: "My Lord — Remember our encounter in Paris where you declared we were friends. It is my duty to send you important information. Milady is on her way to England to kill the duke. Detain her if you can."

The message was sent immediately and the men turned their attentions to matters of war. After two weeks, the messenger returned with a note. "Thank you for your warning. Rest easy. She is being held prisoner at my home," it said.

But even with Milady gone and under the watchful eyes of Lord de Winter, her spirit haunted the dreams of D'Artagnan and Athos. They knew the extent of her power, and could not feel entirely safe.

The Musketeers waited for news from England, but none came. When it did arrive, it was bad. The duke had been assassinated by one of Lord de Winter's guards. The Musketeers also learned that Milady had somehow managed to escape from England and return to France.

"Once again she has seduced someone into joining her evil plans," muttered Athos. "The guard must have helped her escape. The poor man must have been so in love with her that she convinced him to kill the duke. Ah, such a treacherous woman! She must be stopped once and for all."

D'Artagnan could not stop worrying about Constance at the convent. He was sure Milady had found out about his love for Constance and would reach her first.

With the duke dead, the battle was nearly over. D'Artagnan prepared himself for his journey to the convent. The Musketeers insisted on joining him.

THE CONVENT

While the Musketeers make their way to the convent, it is time to find out what became of Milady on her return to France. When she arrived, she sent word to the cardinal to meet her at the convent. She then made her way there.

Once again, she adopted her charming ways to convince the abbess she was a weary traveller who needed a place to stay. "I have been persecuted by the cardinal," she wept. "Please provide me with shelter."

"I see," said the abbess, who was never a supporter of the cardinal. "This is a sad story. Another woman here has suffered like you at the hands of the cardinal. Perhaps you should meet her. I shall bring her to you, for she could use a friend."

The abbess sent for the young lady. Imagine Milady's pleasure in seeing that it was Constance who entered the room. Now she would have D'Artagnan in her power!

As they talked over the next few days, Milady pretended to be a sympathetic friend. Poor Constance had never met Milady and in her innocence trusted her with everything. She spoke many times of her trials with the cardinal and her love for D'Artagnan.

In time, Milady convinced Constance that the only way she could be reunited with D'Artagnan was to leave the convent with her.

Before their carriage arrived, D'Artagnan and his companions galloped into the courtyard.

Milady told Constance it was the cardinal's guards who had arrive to capture them and convinced her to drink some wine for fortification — but it was poisoned!

Milady then rushed out of the room missing D'Artagnan's arrival by mere seconds.

"Constance!" he cried as he entered. But his joy turned to concern. Constance was obviously dying.

"Who did this!" he shouted. He saw the empty glass by her side. "Who poured your wine?"

"It was my friend," said Constance, growing weaker. "She was called Milady." She grasped his arm. "Do not leave me now. I am dying." With those words she fell to the ground and said no more.

D'Artagnan uttered a cry of pain. Athos, Porthos and Aramis came into the room to see what had happened. "Milady must pay for this!" said D'Artagnan, with tears in his eyes. "We must go and find her."

THE END OF MILADY

All four men were possessed by one thought alone — to find Milady. Before they left, however, Athos said he had a short mission to make. He returned in two hours with a mysterious man disguised in a long cloak and spoke to no one.

The group rode at top speed following Milady's trail, making inquiries along the way. They were told that a lady had travelled to a town called Armentieres and was now waiting in an abandoned house at the river for a boat to carry her to freedom.

They wasted no time in reaching the house. The four Musketeers confronted Milady with a list of her unspeakable crimes — the murder of the lovely Constance Bonacieux, the attempted murder of the Comte de Wardes and plotting the death of the Duke of Buckingham.

Milady looked at the men with hatred in her eyes. "You are not a court of law. I defy you to carry on this way."

"Silence!" The man in the cloak spoke.

"Who are you?" asked Milady.

"I am the executioner," he replied.

"Oh have mercy," she cried, as she fell to the floor.

"I think not Madame," said Athos.

Milady nearly fainted from terror. The executioner placed her in a boat and took her to the other side of the river. The men saw the blade of a sword rise and fall in the moonlight. The executioner returned alone.

THE CARDINAL LEARNS ALL

D'Artagnan and the Musketeers returned to Paris with heavy hearts.

Shortly after his arrival, D'Artagnan was arrested and taken to see the cardinal.

"Do you know why I have arrested you?" asked the cardinal. "You are charged with conspiring with the enemy, keeping state secrets and interfering with the cardinal's plans."

"Who charges me?" inquired D'Artagnan. "Was it Milady de Winter? If so, she is dead." D'Artagnan told the cardinal the whole tale.

"So you have tried and punished a woman without permission," said the cardinal. "You shall be arrested for that."

"Sir, I must tell you that we had a letter of pardon."

"Who signed this?" demanded the cardinal. "The king?"

D'Artagnan presented the cardinal with the valuable piece of paper that Athos had forced from Milady. The cardinal read it aloud. He then looked at D'Artagnan and realized that he had no choice but to free him.

This man is young and brave and has much to offer the country, he thought to himself. It is time to put an end to our quarrel.

He was also secretly pleased to know that Milady was dead. She was a dangerous accomplice. The cardinal tore up the letter and proceeded to write another.

"I am lost," thought D'Artagnan, as he received the note. But to his surprise, it was a lieutenant's commission in the Musketeers! But the name had been left blank.

"Do with this as you wish," said the cardinal.

D'Artagnan offered each of his friends the commission in turn.

All three refused, saying it was his. Athos took the letter of commission and with a flourish, filled in D'Artagnan's name. "Dear friend," said Athos. "No one is more worthy than you."

D'Artagnan beamed with pleasure. For the first time in his life he felt he truly deserved to be a Musketeer.

"All for one and one for all!" he shouted with joy.

"All for one and one for all!" the Musketeers repeated together.